At Home

Contents

written by Julie Ellis

Coral reefs look like beautiful underwater gardens. They are made in warm seas by tiny animals called coral polyps. As old coral polyps die, new coral polyps grow on top of them.
Coral reefs take thousands of years to grow.

coral reef

Some reefs grow close to land. Barrier reefs grow further out to sea. Coral atolls grow in a ring shape on top of old volcanoes. Coral reefs are found in clear, shallow water because hard corals need sunlight to grow.

All coral reefs are different, but most reefs have a low island, with a beautiful sandy beach. Close to the beach is a saltwater lake called a lagoon. Further out is the reef edge.

Large coral grows on the edge of the reef. Different animals live in parts of the reef at different times. There are not many fish in the lagoon at low tide, but at high tide they move back in.

lagoon

The largest coral reef in the world is the Great Barrier Reef in Australia. It is made up of about three thousand coral reefs and islands.

Many plants, fish, and other animals live there.
Dolphins and whales swim in the warm water.
There is plenty of food for many different animals.

dolphin

There are two types of coral, growing in many shapes and sizes. Hard corals are very strong. Some grow flat and others grow branches.

hard coral

8

Soft corals are easily damaged. Some are fan-shaped and some grow like branches on a tree. Others grow like bushes. They all have beautiful colors.

soft coral

9

butterflyfish

Divers can watch many colorful fish on coral reefs. Some fish, like sharks, live alone, and some live in schools. Butterflyfish move around in schools. They are friendly and will follow divers. Parrotfish use their special teeth to break off bits of coral to eat.

clownfish

Clownfish are easy to see because of their bright colors. Divers won't go too close to stonefish because they are very poisonous.
When pufferfish feel frightened, they quickly puff up to double their size.

Many other animals live in, on, or around the coral reef. A seahorse can keep safe by staying still and holding on with its tail. Jellyfish and octopuses move around with sea snakes, eels, and starfish.

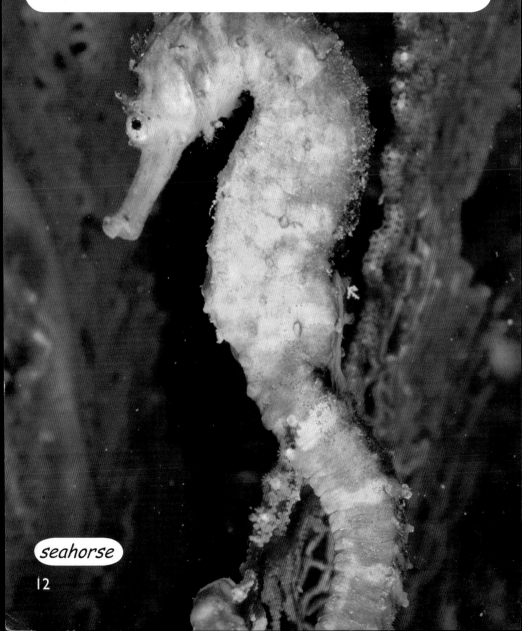

seahorse

sea turtle

Turtles live in coral reefs and lay their eggs in the sand on the beach. Crabs and lobsters hide in coral to keep safe from hungry fish and sea birds. Giant clams are easy to see because of their size.

13

Some plants and animals live on a reef for all of their lives. Many animals find food and shelter there, and they all need one another. A change in one part of the food chain will change the coral reef.

reef shark

If there are not enough sharks, there will be too many fish. If there are too many fish, there will not be enough coral. Then every other plant and animal will die or go away.

divers

Many people visit coral reefs because they are so beautiful. Coral reefs can teach us a lot about fish and other animals and how they live together.